I Don't Live Here!
by Pam Conrad

illustrated by Diane de Groat

E. P. DUTTON   NEW YORK

The lines quoted on page 56 are reprinted from *Lord Dragonfly* by William Heyen by permission of the publisher, Vanguard Press, Inc. Copyright © 1981 by William Heyen.

Library of Congress Cataloging in Publication Data

Conrad, Pam.
 I don't live here!

 Summary: Eight-year-old Nicki believes she will never be happy in the large old house her family has moved to, even if it does have a gazebo in the yard.
 1. Children's stories, American. [1. Moving, Household—Fiction. 2. Family life—Fiction
I. de Groat, Diane, ill. II. Title
PZ7.C76476Iad 1984 [Fic] 84-8040
ISBN 0-525-44080-1

Published in the United States by E. P. Dutton, Inc., 2 Park Avenue, New York, N.Y. 10016

Published simultaneously in Canada by
Fitzhenry & Whiteside Limited, Toronto

Designer: Julia Gran

Printed in the U.S.A.   W   First Edition
10 9 8 7 6 5 4 3 2 1

for Johanna who spins webs,
and for Sarah who eats honeysuckle

1

No One's Allowed on Nicki's Swing

Nicki Bennet woke up before her eyes did that morning. She could feel her sheet wrapped tightly around one leg, but she didn't move. She could feel her hair stretched across her nose, but she was very still.

Summer was the best—nothing to hurry for, nothing to rush about. Slowly, she opened her eyes and groaned. She had forgotten that she wasn't in her old familiar room. She was in the new house, and her happy summertime feeling slipped away.

She would never like it here. The bedroom her parents had picked for her was too ugly, the kitchen downstairs was too yellow, and the yard was just too big. They'd been here only one day, and already Nicki missed the old neighborhood where she had spent all eight years of her life so far. She missed her good old house, where her best friend, Lisa, was only three houses away.

Nicki wasn't even near the bathroom in this house. It was all the way down the hall. Well, if she had an accident, it wouldn't be her fault, she thought as she padded out of her room. And whoever heard of a bathtub with feet?

She stared at the bathtub sleepily. If a bathtub had feet, then the drain must be its mouth, and the knobs were its wiggly eyes, and then the water must run out its nose to fill the tub. Yuk. What a dumb bathroom. Everything in this house was stupid.

She stood up and glanced out the window. At first she thought she was dreaming. She rubbed her eyes real hard and looked again. She wasn't dreaming. There really *was* a boy swinging on the old swing set in the backyard. He was just sitting there, all alone, swinging back and forth, back and forth.

She tore down the hall to her room and began ripping open the packed boxes. Where were her shorts? Her T-shirts? She pulled on her wrinkled clothes from yesterday and ran back to the window to look again. He was still there. Who was he? Nicki wanted to check this kid out before anyone else discovered him.

Nicki ran quietly down the hall. She could hear her mother humming somewhere. Her little sister, Shirley, was still asleep in her own room. No one saw her to ask where she was going. Nicki ran down the stairs, through the house, and out the back door, slowing her step as she came down the back steps. She walked casually across the lawn, past the birdbath, and sat on the swing beside the boy.

They looked at each other.

"This is my swing," she said.

"It's Mrs. Templeton's swing. She always lets me swing on it."

"Well, we bought this house from Mrs. Templeton, and that included the swings and the grass and the whole thing."

Silence.

Nicki challenged him. "Well?"

"I think you're in a period of adjustment," he said, looking at her calmly.

"A what?"

He shrugged. "It's probably hard to get used to a new house and a new neighborhood. This is your period of adjustment. My mother said it might be rough in the beginning."

"Hey!" Nicki jumped up and faced him, her hands on her hips. She wished she had on her T-shirt with King Kong on the front. "I said, 'This is my swing,'

3

and no one's allowed on unless they get permission from me. Get it?"

The boy stood up slowly and tucked his hands into his back pockets. "Okay, okay." He backed off and watched her.

"Well? What are you looking at?" she demanded.

"I'm curious to see how you're going to swing on all four of those swings at the same time." At that, he laughed a ridiculous laugh, turned, and ran a-cross the lawn, disappearing behind the house next door.

Nicki was furious, and she had nowhere to run. She didn't even have her safe old room anymore. She turned and ran in the opposite direction, over the smooth green lawn to the back of the yard, and into the . . . What had her mother called it? Oh, yes, the gazebo. What a stupid name, but it was as good a place as any for being alone, for getting away from a creepy boy.

She threw herself on the floor and looked carefully around at the gazebo. She had never been in one before. It was just like a room, only it was outdoors. There was a step up to a wooden floor, a pointed roof with an old gray hornets' nest way up at the tip, and the walls went only halfway up. All around, there were windows without glass or screens, just big open windows—like windows *should* be, Nicki thought.

"I don't have to put up with this new kid," she

mumbled. "I won't stay here. I'll move back to the old neighborhood, and I'll live in Lisa's garage if I have to. I'll even fix my own food." She could make salads. Nicki looked around and found leaves and some tiny flowers and a little dirt. Also some sticks. At first she arranged all the things in a design in the center of a large leaf, and then she mashed them all into a pulp. Delicious!

"Nicki!" It was her mother calling.

"What?"

"What are you doing out there? Come on in and comb your hair and brush your teeth and . . ."

Her mother's voice faded behind the banging of the screen door. Nicki left the mush salad on the step to the gazebo and walked slowly back to the house and into the kitchen. Shirley was sitting at the table, eating a small bowl of colorful cereal.

Her father came whistling down what he called "the servant's staircase." It was all wooden and dusty and echoey. "Hi, kiddo," he said, smiling at Nicki. "How are you doing? You enjoying the new house?"

"No."

"Isn't it great?"

"No."

"This is going to be a wonderful summer."

Nicki rolled her eyes. He wasn't listening. Wasn't that typical? He was so excited, he didn't even hear her.

"Did you meet any neighborhood kids yet?"

"No." She thought of that dumb boy. He didn't count.

"You'll meet them. Have no fear."

"I want to go home," Nicki suddenly announced to her father.

He sat down at the table and made room in front of him. "This *is* home, Nicki. This is our house now. Your bed is upstairs, and soon you'll have all your toys unpacked, all the curtains will be up, and you won't even remember what the other house looked like."

"My room has a purple rug," Shirley announced.

Boy, was she dumb. All excited about a rug.

"It's bright purple like a big, juicy plum."

Nicki rolled her eyes. "Yeah, well, my rug is gray like the driveway, and my ceiling is white like a cloudy day, and my walls are flowery like an old tissue box."

Her mother laughed and set a mug of coffee in front of Mr. Bennet. "Do you want to paint your room a new color, Nicki? What color would you like?"

"I don't care. I'm not staying here long enough to bother, so it doesn't matter."

"Where's she going?" Shirley asked her mother.

"Nowhere, Shirley. Don't worry. Nicki just has to get used to our new house, that's all."

"This isn't a 'new' house," Nicki said. "It's an old house, an old, *old* house."

"That's right," her father said. "That's why your mother and I bought it, and I think, *eventually,* we'll all be happy here."

Nicki kept her mouth shut. She would never like it here, but she knew there was no use saying it again.

"You go on upstairs now, Nicki," her mother said, "and find some clean clothes and wash up. After breakfast, I want you to unpack all those boxes in your room. Your dresser is empty. Your toy box and shelves are empty."

Nicki's father reached out and squeezed her hand. "You know, if you fix up your room, it will begin to feel more like home to you. Like a bird building a nest, or a wild coyote marking out its territory. You make your mark, and it's your own special place."

It was hopeless. They just wouldn't believe her until she was really gone. She *couldn't* unpack her boxes. She would be taking them to Lisa's when she moved out.

"Go on now," her father said, nudging her towards the door. "Go see what you can do up there." He nudged her right out of the kitchen.

2

Spiderweb

Nicki stood in the doorway of her new room and sighed. There was nothing good about this room. Nothing. The closet was big enough to hide in, and the doorknobs almost had faces in their funny swirly designs, but that wasn't much.

She went in, put her pillow at the top of her bed, and pulled the Charlie Brown sleeping bag up over it, smoothing and tugging until it looked pretty neat. Then she threw herself on it. Her father had piled the boxes and crates along one wall. Maybe she should look through the boxes and just take what she really needed when she moved to Lisa's.

A ball of string sat on top of one of the crates. It was fat, loads and loads of string. I wonder, she thought, if it would reach all the way to Lisa's house?

She got up and tied the end of the string to the top knob on her dresser and walked across the room. It looked like a tightrope.

She wrapped the string around the knob at the foot of her bed and pulled it tight. Then, she walked across to her desk and wove the string through the back of her desk chair. The letter *L*.

Could she make a square? She walked across the room and tied the string to the radiator, then pulled more string out and tied it back again on the top knob of the dresser. A boxing ring! She put the ball of string down and began throwing punches into the air at imaginary partners. *Pow! Pow!* She threw punches, ducked, swung, and jumped. The champion, the great Nicki Bennet!

She picked up the string again and walked diagonally to the desk. The square was now cut into two triangles. Very neat. *Too* neat. Closing her eyes, she threw the ball up into the air. It landed by her dresser. She tied it to a different knob and threw it again.

The string stuck on the ceiling light, and the ball fell back at her feet. Wonderful! She rolled the ball of string across her bed. It fell between the wall and the mattress. She climbed underneath and pulled the ball out.

Back and forth went the ball, over her desk, under the radiator, around her dresser, on top of the curtain rods, beneath her closet door and out over the top, around doorknobs and bedknobs, and window latches, when at last the ball of string rolled across the floor and disappeared into just a long string that came to an end.

Nicki smiled. There! Now the room looked much better.

Shirley stood in the doorway, bug-eyed. "What are you playing?" she asked.

Nicki admired her creation. "I'm playing a string game."

"Looks like you're playing spider to me."

Yes! Nicki looked around. It did look like a spider-web, didn't it? She closed her eyes and stretched out her arms, touching the strings gently with her hands.

"I'll be the spider, Shirl, and you be the fly. See if you can come through, and I'll see if I can feel my web move."

She could hear Shirley begin creeping along the floor. "Ooooo!" Nicki wailed. "Sounds like an old beetle to me!" She threw herself on top of Shirley, and they both squealed and screeched, rolling around beneath the web of knots and string. The rest of the

morning they walked their Barbie dolls across the tightropes, in and out of trouble and danger.

"Nicki." Suddenly her father was there. "Nicki," he said, shaking his head. "No one is going to unpack for you. Is that clear?"

"Yes, Dad."

"Not your mother. Not me. *You* have to do it."

"I know."

"And no one's going to clean up this string mess for you either."

They looked at each other a long minute. "Come down now and have lunch," he said, and then he turned and walked away. Nicki and Shirley sat quietly in the middle of the room, surrounded by miles and miles of wrapped-up, knotted-up string. They smiled at each other.

"Want me to unpack for you?" Shirley whispered.

"Nah," said Nicki. But she couldn't tell Shirley why. A five-year-old just wouldn't understand.

"Tell you what, though. I'll race you downstairs. You take the servant's staircase, and I'll take the red stairs. Meet you in the kitchen."

They both scrambled along the floor beneath the web, out the hall, and down the two staircases. Nicki's feet went without a sound on the thick red carpet, and Shirley's feet banged on each hard, creaking step in the narrow staircase that opened out into the kitchen.

Shirley won. Nicki filed away in her head for later which staircase would get her downstairs quickest.

Their mother was standing in the middle of the room with a tray in her hands. "Girls, I need some help. Shirley, get the napkins, and Nicki, bring that pitcher of lemonade along with you. We're going to have lunch on the porch. Won't that be nice?"

"It doesn't matter," Nicki said. "Nothing matters to me."

Her mother sighed and left the kitchen, carrying her tray of cold cuts and paper plates. Shirley followed behind.

The large pitcher of lemonade stood on the kitchen table among boxes and wrappings and cleaners. Nicki dipped her finger into it and touched the ice cubes. They felt cool and slippery. She slipped her finger into her mouth. It tasted a bit like the leaf salad she had made in the gazebo that morning.

Oh, well. She wiped her finger on her shorts, lifted the cool, wet pitcher, and followed the direction her mother had taken. She wasn't even sure how to get to the porch from the kitchen. This house was too big. She knew her way around the old house. It was so easy to live there.

The screened porch ran around two sides of the new house. Nicki checked it out, thinking about how easily she could hide here, on one side or the other.

"Come on, Nicki," her mother said. "Sit here, and

we'll have some sandwiches and lemonade together. And then I have to get back to work."

"Me, too," said Mr. Bennet. "Boy, it's hot today, isn't it?" He pulled off his T-shirt and wiped his neck with it.

"I miss Lisa," Nicki said, collapsing into her seat.

She saw her parents look at each other, and her mother said in her patient voice, "Well, why don't you call her up and invite her for a visit?"

Why hadn't Nicki thought of that? Of course, and then she and Lisa could work up a plan for her to move into Lisa's garage. Nicki bolted from the table, ran through the house and out into the kitchen.

"After lunch," her mother called, but Nicki pretended she hadn't heard. She knew Lisa's phone number by heart. The phone rang and rang. Finally, Mrs. Wessley answered.

"Hello?"

"Hi, Mrs. Wessley. Is Lisa there?"

"Who is this?"

"It's me, Nicki."

"Why, goodness, Nicki! How are you? How are you enjoying your new house?"

"It stinks. Is Lisa there?"

"Oh, I'll bet you make friends in no time."

"Yeah. Is Lisa home?"

"I haven't seen her, Nicki. She went out on her bike this morning, and she hasn't been back since.

I'm sure she'll be home soon. Do you want me to have her call you?"

Nicki felt disappointed. Her best friend wasn't even missing her. She was out playing just as if it were any old day. "I want her to come visit me. Can she come today?"

Mrs. Wessley paused. "Well, not today, but how about a week from Friday? She can visit you for the afternoon then, if you like."

"Oh, okay." Nicki sighed. That was nearly two weeks off, but it would give her some time to work out a good plan for leaving.

Nicki hung up and wrote on the calendar a week from Friday: *Lisa visits.* And *that* will be the day I move out, she thought.

3

Letting Him Swing

Nicki sat on the back steps playing Chinese jacks. She was bored. All the boxes in her room were still sealed, except for the one that held her shorts and shirts. She'd opened that one and pulled clothes out of it each morning. But the spiderweb was still there, and her parents said again that her room was her responsibility. They said they wouldn't even set foot in her room until she straightened it up.

Nicki threw the jacks on the ground. She would never take the string down. That way no grown-ups could ever walk through without getting their glasses or their hair clips all tangled and stuck.

"Hi."

Nicki looked up to see that boy standing at the bottom of the steps. She stared at him. He waited.

"You want to play soccer?" he asked. He had a grass-stained soccer ball between his sneakers.

"Nah."

"Okay." He turned and kicked the ball over the lawn and across the driveway into the next yard. He went after it, and she watched him, feeling sad that he left so quickly. Maybe he wasn't too bad. Maybe he'd be an all right friend, at least for a week or so, until she was ready to leave.

She picked up her colorful plastic rings, slipped them in her pocket, walked casually over to the swing, and sat on the end seat.

"You're allowed to swing on my swing today," she shouted. He kicked the ball twice around the bush. She wondered if he hadn't heard her, or if he *had* heard her, maybe he didn't want to swing now. She began to pump high, pretending not to care if he came over or not.

With one mighty kick, he lifted the ball into the air, and it came down right in the center of the bush. He turned, trotted over, and sat on the swing right beside her. His T-shirt said BACKWARDS backwards, right across his chest, and he had a ballpoint tattoo of an anchor on the back of his hand.

"What's your name anyway?" he asked.

"Nicki Bennet."

"I'm Jeffrey Reynolds. I live in that house over there." He motioned with his chin to the house next to Nicki's. "We moved here from Boston two years ago, and I had a dog there, but he died."

"How old are you?" she asked.

"Nine," he answered. "How old are you? Seven?"

"I'm eight and a half," she lied. The half was the lie.

"Can you jump off the swing when it's really high?" he wanted to know. "Watch."

He held on to the chains, and as he swung higher and higher, he inched his bottom forward on the seat. When the swing pitched, he let go of the chains and flew through the air, landing on his hands and knees in the grass, way out in front of the swings. Nicki loved him instantly.

He turned and watched. There was no getting out of it. One, she told herself, two, three! She let go of the chains and soared through the air, landing in the grass by his side. They laughed, and he pushed her down.

"Come on," he said, and ran up into the gazebo. As he sat down on the step, he popped a flower into his mouth.

"What are you *doing*?" she asked.

"Honeysuckle," he said. "See?" He pulled another flower off the vine that circled the door of the gazebo.

Then he carefully snapped the base of it and drew out a long, white stalk from inside. A drop of moisture formed on the end, clear and sweet.

"Taste," he said. Nicki let the drop fall on her tongue.

"Mmmmmm! That's great. Like candy." She sat down next to him and snapped off another blossom.

"What grade are you going into?" he asked.

"Third," she said.

"I'm going into fourth. I hate school."

"Yeah," she agreed. "Me, too."

"Did you know there's a nursery school around the block here in a big old house? Come on. I'll show you. But listen," he whispered, "we have to sneak up, all right? Can you sneak? Are you real quiet?"

Years of lurking and prowling and hiding were finally paying off, as if it had all been in preparation for this very day. "Yeah, I can sneak."

"Let's go." Jeffrey crept through his backyard, through the raspberry patch. The thorns stuck on their shorts and shirts, and scratched their legs, but they were both brave, unwilling to stop for such minor problems.

Nicki followed him closely. His steps were silent. She knew how to do that perfectly. When they reached the fence, he turned and put his finger to his lips. "Shhh." Holding his hands together, he signaled her to step into them, and he hoisted her over the

fence. This she had never done before, but she was pleased that she did it expertly.

He scrambled over the fence after her without the help of a boost, and continued to lead the way. Nicki looked back at her house. She would have to remember this, and take Shirley later.

Jeffrey signaled Nicki to crawl, and they both got down on their hands and knees and continued on. They passed a garage, a compost heap, a tomato patch, and an unfamiliar back stoop until they arrived at an area of overgrown weeds and bushes.

"Here it is," Jeffrey whispered, but Nicki knew that already. She could hear children playing and shouting. They parted the weeds and found themselves on the very edge of a play yard, behind a chain link fence. There were wooden climbing toys and sling swings and a million little kids and a few teachers.

"What are you doing here?" a voice demanded. Nicki froze, and then realized a teacher was talking to one of the small children. Nicki and Jeffrey smiled at each other in relief and watched the kids.

"Hey, you know what?" Jeffrey leaned close to Nicki. He smelled like soap and maple syrup. "Do you want to play spies?"

"Sure." That sounded great.

"Then go back to your house and get some paper and two pencils."

Nicki looked at him. She wasn't used to being

bossed around. She was usually the boss. "Why don't you?"

"I'll keep guard" was his answer. "You go ahead."

Nicki frowned. She would do it this time, but next time, he would. And at that, she turned and retraced her steps back to her house.

4

Jeffrey and Webber

Nicki stormed up the back steps two at a time, yelling, "I need some paper and pencils!"

"Whatever for?" Her mother was sitting at the kitchen table drinking coffee and filling out forms. "Wait a minute. Wait a minute," she protested. "You can't have that pencil. I'm using it right now. Let me help you find others."

"I met a friend," Nicki told her.

"Great. Does she live near here?"

"It's a boy," Nicki said, not looking at her mother.

"He lives next door. Jeffrey. He used to live in Boston, and he had a dog, but it died."

"What are the pencils for?"

"We're playing school," Nicki fibbed.

Her mother handed her a small pad and two long yellow pencils. "Here you go." Nicki was out the back door when she heard her mother call, "Have fun," and then softer, "Be good."

She followed the route back to the nursery school. When she got to the fence, she threw the paper and pencils over and hopped over easily.

She thought she could sneak up on Jeffrey, but he turned and looked at her as soon as she came into view.

"Did you get some?"

She held the pad and pencils before her and smiled.

"Good." He took them from her, and she took them back, split the pad in half, and kept the longest pencil for herself.

"Now what?" she asked.

"Well, you see, we have to find out what their names are, and their behavior patterns."

"Their what?"

"Let me show you. See that kid over there on the swing?"

"Hmmmm."

"Well, watch. His name is Thomas. Watch him."

The little boy, smaller than Shirley, held on to the swing and rocked back and forth. Every once in a

25

while, his eyes closed, and his head bobbed down. Nicki and Jeffrey stifled their giggles.

Jeffrey wrote on his pad: *Thomas, little, red shorts, very sleepy.*

"How do you know his name?"

"Listen to the teachers," he told her.

One called, "Alisa! Alisa! Come down off there now. That's much too high."

Aha! Nicki wrote on her pad: *Alisa, medium, Disneyland shirt, brave.*

"What are you doing here?" A little boy stood looking at them through the fence. Their cover was blown.

"Get out of here," Jeffrey said. "We're undercover spies. Get lost before you're sorry."

"What's your name?" The kid kicked the fence. How would they get rid of this pest? If they talked to him, the teachers might see, and tell them to leave.

"If we tell you, will you go back to playing?"

"Yeah."

"I'm Jeffrey. Now get lost."

"What's *your* name?" the kid asked, wrapping his fingers around the chain link fence. Nicki could tell he was never going to leave. There was probably some law about spying on nursery schools, Nicki thought. It would be better—more like a real spy—not to give him her real name.

"What's your name, girl?" he asked louder.

She shrugged. "Whatever," she answered.

"What? What did you say? Webber?"

"Yeah, Webber." She and Jeffrey exchanged a glance.

"Mrs. Marsh! Mrs. Marsh!"

Nicki and Jeffrey turned and flew through the weeds on hands and knees until they could no longer be seen. They sat crouched in the tall grass, listening.

"Yes, Archie, what do you want, dear?" They could hear the teacher walk over to the fence.

"Jeffrey and Webber just ran away."

"What, Archie?"

"There were just two spies here, Jeffrey and Webber. They ran away."

"Is that right, Archie? My, my, my. Come on back to the sandbox, dear. There are lots of friends for you to play with over there. You don't have to look for anyone in the bushes." Nicki smiled. She could tell that the teacher thought Jeffrey and Webber were imaginary, kind of like the little giraffe that Shirley talked about sometimes.

"Come on," Nicki whispered. She led the way back home, creeping quietly ahead of Jeffrey. When they got to the fence, she clasped her hands together and signaled him to step up. He did, and then he watched as she climbed over after him.

"You're good, for a girl," he told her.

Nicki ran ahead before he could see her smile. She felt shy and pleased at the same time.

"Psssst!"

She stopped and looked back. "Have a snack," he said. He threw a raspberry at her, and she caught it. What a wonderful day this was!

She popped the berry in her mouth and then spit it out. "Yuk, it's all fuzzy." He ignored her, stuffing his mouth with more and more berries. She ran back to the gazebo to get some honeysuckle.

Jeffrey soon joined her and stretched out on the wooden floor. "You're lucky to have a clubhouse," he said.

"It's not a clubhouse," she corrected. "It's a gazebo."

"A gazebo? That's what my father calls my Aunt Madeline, an old gazebo."

"Well, that's what gazebo means, I guess," said Nicki. "Something that's very, very old, like about a hundred years or something."

He suddenly pointed to her legs. "You're bleeding, Nicki. Look at that."

Nicki looked at the tiny trails of blood that were running down her legs from the raspberry scratches.

"So are you," she told him.

They both examined their legs closely. Blood was so interesting. Nicki let a drop fall onto a honeysuckle flower.

"Want to be blood brothers?" he asked.

"How about blood sisters?" she answered.

He frowned. "Maybe it should be blood neighbors."

"I don't know," she answered. "I'm not staying here much longer. Just till next Friday."

"Well, then, how about blood spies? A secret club?"

"Okay," she agreed, and slid closer to him and held out her leg. He twisted himself until his calf was touching hers, and their two scratches met.

"I now declare us blood spies," he said in a serious voice. "Always faithful, always brave, ready to help each other, no matter what. You say, 'I solemnly swear.' "

"I solemnly swear."

They sat quiet then, apart, sucking on the flowers. And then he asked, "What do you mean, you're leaving next Friday? You just moved here."

Nicki pulled a leaf from the honeysuckle vine and wiped the blood off her leg. "My best friend from my old house is coming then, and I'm going to sneak home with her and live in her garage."

Jeffrey's eyes widened. "Really?"

"Yep."

"Does anybody know?"

"Nope. Just you, right now."

"Can I help?"

Nicki narrowed her eyes and looked at him.

"You can trust me," he told her. "We're blood spies."

"I'll think about it. I haven't come up with an

30

escape plan yet, but you might be able to help some-
how. I'll think about it."

"Jeffrey!"

"That's my mother," he said, looking over the railing of the gazebo. "Better go. See you later, Webber."

He jumped up and ran across the lawn to his house.
Nicki sat watching him until she heard the screen
door slam. Yes. It might be good to include him in
her plan.

5

The Escape Plan

A week later, Nicki and Jeffrey sat cross-legged on the floor of the gazebo, sharing a bag of cold bagels as they had done each morning. It was Thursday. Tomorrow Lisa was coming for a visit, and Nicki would be leaving.

"Why don't you put anything on these, like jelly or something?" Jeffrey asked.

"I like them plain." Nicki bit hers. It was hard enough sneaking the bagels out of the house without having to bring jelly and a knife, too.

"What's the weirdest thing you ever ate?" he asked.

She thought a minute. "My sister made dinner once, and she's only five, and she made bologna sandwiches with pickles and maraschino cherries, with colored toothpicks stuck in the top."

Jeffrey shivered. "Ugh."

"How about you? What's the weirdest thing you ever ate?"

"Worms," he told her.

"You're kidding!"

"No, I really did."

Nicki watched his face. He didn't seem to be lying.

"How's your plan going?" he asked. "Are you all ready to leave tomorrow?"

She bit off a hunk of bagel and chewed. "Well, I've got a few things packed, and I have an idea about how I could do it, but . . . I don't know. . . ." She looked at him sideways.

"What's the matter?"

"I'm not sure I can trust you."

"What do you think? That I'm going to tell?"

"How do I know you won't?"

"We're blood spies. I told you!"

"Not good enough."

He thought a minute. "You mean you want me to prove myself?"

"Yeah." She hadn't thought of that, but that sounded good. "Okay, prove yourself."

"How about if I eat a worm?"

She shivered. "You mean you'd eat a worm now?"

"Yeah, if you promise to let me in on your plan, I'll eat a worm for you. Then you'll know you can trust me. You don't tell my mother I eat worms, and I don't tell your mother you're leaving."

"Okay," Nicki said in a small voice. "But where do we find worms?"

Jeffrey got up. "Let's go look. I think Mrs. Templeton had a compost heap back here behind the garage."

"What's a compost heap?"

"It's just a pile of leaves and clippings left to rot."

He picked up a long stick and jabbed a mound of leaves and dirt with it. "See?"

"Yes, but what's it for?" Nicki picked up another stick and poked the pile gently.

"I'm not sure. It's got something to do with gardening, but look! See?"

He lifted the stick in the air and draped over it, like a fat string of spaghetti on a fork, hung a worm.

"Aaaaaa!" Nicki backed off in horror. "That's disgusting! Put it back!"

"No, I'm going to *eat* it," he said. "Watch!"

Nicki stood there, both hands clapped over her mouth in terror.

"Promise me you'll let me in on your escape plans?"

"Yes. Yes."

He held it over his mouth and stuck his tongue way out. "And you'll let me help?"

"Sure." She nodded faintly, the hair on the back of her neck prickling her collar.

"Promise?"

"Promise."

"Blood spies' honor?"

"Blood spies' honor."

He jerked the stick and the fat, wet worm dropped into his open mouth. Nicki shrieked, and Jeffrey made a loud, noisy gulp, and then wiped some pretend sweat off his forehead.

"Whew!" he said.

Nicki's arms hung at her sides. "Oh," she whispered. "I'm so glad you didn't chew it."

"Well," he said casually, tossing the stick onto the compost heap, "tell me your plan now."

She followed him back to the gazebo, where he sat down and began nibbling on another bagel. "Shoot," he said.

"Well, it's pretty simple, I guess. Lisa's coming for the afternoon, and I have a box in my room that's packed with all the things I'll need when I live there: some clothes, my Lego toys, my back scratcher—"

"Yeah, so how do you get that to Lisa's?"

"Lisa's mother will come for her at dinnertime, and we'll get her to come in and talk to my mother."

"I get it. And while she's talking, you'll hide the box in the car."

"Not only that, but *I'll* hide in the car, too. Lisa has a station wagon, so I'll lie down in the way back."

"Won't Lisa's mother see you when she gets in the car?"

"Nah. Their car is a wreck, and there are always sleeping bags and stuff in the back that I can hide under."

"Won't your mother go after you once she sees you're gone?"

Nicki frowned. "Once I'm at Lisa's, I'll worry about that. First thing, I have to *get* there."

"Sounds like it might work, Webber, except for one thing."

"What?"

"Won't your mother expect you to say good-bye to Lisa and be standing there at the curb waving when they drive away?"

"Hmmmm. I hadn't thought of that."

"Unless—" His eyebrows bobbed up and down.

"What?"

"I can be a kind of a decoy. When Lisa leaves, I can make it look like you're too busy playing with me to say good-bye. I'll sit out in the gazebo and make a racket, and your friend can say she already said good-bye to you, and by the time your mother discovers you're gone, you'll be at Lisa's."

"Yeah! That would work. And you would do that? Make noise in the gazebo like we're playing?"

"Do you doubt the word of a blood spy?"

Nicki glanced at his mouth and thought of the worm. "Not for a minute, Jeffrey. Not for a minute."

6

Lisa Visits

Nicki and Shirley sat on the front stoop waiting for Lisa to arrive. Nicki was so happy and excited that she hugged her sister.

"Lisa's coming! Lisa's coming!" she said over and over, smiling and watching each car that passed.

"So?" Shirley was very quiet.

"Lisa's my *best friend.*" Suddenly, Nicki realized that Shirley must be missing somebody, too, and asked, "Who's *your* best friend, Shirl?"

"You are."

"No, I don't mean a sister or a family person. I mean best friend, somebody you miss now from the other house."

Shirley thought a minute. "I guess I miss Elmo most of all."

"But Elmo's a dog."

"Well, that's who I miss most of all. I miss a nice dog who likes to run next to me and lick my face. Do you think Mommy will let Elmo visit me here one day? Like Lisa?"

"I don't think so," said Nicki. "I never heard of a dog visiting an old friend."

Shirley looked so sad that Nicki felt a strange tugging inside. She would really miss Shirley. "But you know what we can do? We can walk around the new neighborhood and find another dog friend for you before I leave. How about that?"

"Before you leave?"

"I mean, you know, before Lisa leaves."

"But I'll always love Elmo. There's nobody like him."

"I know. I know. Tell you what, when Lisa comes, she can help us find a dog friend for you. We'll all go looking for one. What do you say?"

A car horn beeped, and the Wessleys' station wagon pulled up at the curb. Lisa jumped out, with her red sneakers and her flying braids, and came running towards them.

"Lisa!"

"Nicki!"

They screamed and shouted. Nicki had never really hugged Lisa before, but now they were hugging and jumping, and they fell down in the grass laughing, just like two best friends.

"Come on in, Lisa. Come on up to my room."

They took off holding hands, with Shirley tagging along. Nicki led the way through the kitchen, up the stairs to her room, and stood proudly in the doorway, excited to hear what Lisa would say about her spiderweb.

"How come you have all this stupid string in here?" Lisa asked, looking in at the room as if it were a mess.

"It's a spiderweb," Shirley explained.

"Shirley, get lost," said Nicki. She was annoyed at Shirley . . . or maybe at Lisa. She wasn't sure who. "Lisa is here to visit *me.* Go on. Go play and leave us alone." She would have to tell Lisa her plan in secret anyway.

"But you said you'd help me find a dog friend." Shirley stood in the doorway with her arms crossed.

"Later, I said. Not now."

"Nicki," her sister whined.

"Ma!" Nicki yelled. "Tell Shirley to leave me alone. She's pestering us."

"Shirley," their mother called from downstairs. "Come on down. Let Nicki and Lisa visit alone for a bit."

Shirley stomped out, mumbling under her breath. Lisa and Nicki smiled at each other and crawled into the room. "This is a spiderweb," Nicki went on to explain, "And it's good for pretending you're a bug."

"Hmmmm, but how is it living here?" Lisa wanted to know, her barrette snagging on a string.

"It's terrible, and my parents refuse to move back, so—"

"I know. They couldn't now anyway. There are new people in your house."

"What? Already?"

"Yes, and they have a cat and a baby, and they put up red curtains in your room."

"Red curtains? Yuk! How could they do that?" Nicki felt awful. Her room. New people just went in and did all different things to her room. A baby even. Messing it all up.

"I went to visit them," Lisa said. "And they let me play in your room. I watched the lady change her baby, and she put little stretch nighties on him, and his crib is right where your bed used to be."

"Yeah? In my room?"

"And the lady said I could come back anytime and visit him in your room. Maybe you could come, too."

Nicki thought she might cry. It wasn't fair. It seemed almost as if her room were Lisa's now, as if it were Lisa who had taken it away from her. And it certainly didn't sound like Lisa was miserable without her. Some best friend! Nicki was all mixed up.

Did she even *want* to go back to the old neighborhood? Suddenly, the escape plan seemed like a ball of knots and confusion.

"Come on," Nicki said. "I told Shirley I'd help her find a friend. She misses old Elmo, and we decided to look for a new dog today." She ran from her room and scooted down the stairs, hoping Lisa wouldn't talk to her for a while about her old house. Their footsteps clattered in the stairway.

Shirley was sitting at the kitchen table, eating a small bowl of chocolate pudding. "Come on," Nicki said, tugging at her arm. "Let's go find that dog now."

"What dog?" asked her mother. "And why are you off so fast?" Why did her mother always ask so many questions?

"There's nothing to do in that dumb room. Come on, Shirley. Do you want to go, or not?"

"Nicki," her mother scolded. "Calm down. Lisa is your guest, so help her find her way around, and let her join in. Do you understand?"

"I will. I will," Nicki said. "Come on. Let's go around the block and see if we can find a dog."

The three of them left the house and started down the back steps. "What's that?" asked Lisa, pointing out towards the gazebo.

"The gazebo," said Shirley.

"Nothing," Nicki said at the same time.

"What's a gazebo?" Lisa wanted to know.

44

"I'll show you later." Nicki headed to the front of the house. "Let's go find a dog."

Shirley and Lisa walked together, and Nicki walked a little bit ahead of them, feeling sad and confused about her old room and about Lisa not really feeling like a best friend anymore. And what about the escape plan?

One neighbor had a sprinkler going, and Nicki just walked right through without even shivering. Lisa and Shirley squealed and ran past her, holding their arms up over their heads.

"What's the matter, Nicki?" Lisa looked back at her.

"Nothing," she said, but inside she thought, Everything, just everything.

7

New Friends

The girls walked up the block, the large maple trees shading them and making patches of dappled sun on the sidewalk. It was a quiet street, no cars, no traffic at all, and Nicki skipped over the curb and walked down the middle of the street alone. It would be a good place for roller skating, no cracks, no lines, just smooth cement.

"Nicki, look!"

Shirley was standing in front of a house, pointing at a large dog who was sitting on the front porch. He was dark brown, and he was chained to the railing.

They stood watching him. He looked back and then made a deep growling noise.

"Ohhhh, Shirley, I don't know," Nicki said. "He doesn't look too friendly to me."

"He's not like Elmo at all," Lisa added.

"You're right." Shirley slipped her hand in Lisa's. "I want a friend like Elmo. Elmo never had to be tied up."

They continued up the block.

"But I don't think you can just *find* a dog," Lisa said. "How can you look for a friend by walking around the block?"

"Well, how else do you find a friend?" Nicki asked. A lot Lisa knew! She didn't know what it was like to have to start all over again.

"I don't know," Lisa said. "But this seems dumb, walking around the block like you expect a friend to appear."

Just then, a big orange yellow dog came bounding up a driveway, barking in a real friendly way. He jumped on each of them and licked the chocolate pudding off Shirley's face.

"I found him!" Shirley squealed, putting her arms around the dog and patting him and rubbing him. His tail wagged so hard, he could hardly stand up. He was the happiest dog Nicki had ever seen.

A man started up the driveway towards them, calling his dog. "Lester! You get back here. Come on."

The big old dog went slinking back to the man's feet, and rolled over on his back.

"Oh, Lester, you old coot." The man rubbed the dog's belly and laughed. "Hi," he said to the girls. "Did old Lester here scare you? He's pretty rambunctious."

"No, he's real nice," Shirley said. "I was just out looking for a friend. I miss Elmo from our old house, and I really need a new friend, someone like Lester here."

The man looked up at them. "Are you new in the neighborhood?"

"Yes, we just moved in," Shirley said. "165 Mitchell Street."

"Ah, the Templeton house. You're our new neighbors. And what's your name?"

"I'm Shirley Bennet, and that's my sister, Nicki. And that's her friend from the old house. She's just visiting. She's not a new neighbor."

"I'm Tom Leighton." He shook Shirley's hand. "How old are you, Nicki? You look like you're my daughter's age."

"I'm eight," she answered, watching Shirley rub Lester's belly and then lie down on the driveway beside him.

Mr. Leighton turned back towards the house. "Katie!" he called. "Come here a minute."

Lisa and Nicki looked at each other, and Nicki smiled knowingly. *This* was how to make a new friend. Then, a skinny girl with Indian bead bracelets came around the house and skipped up to her father.

"Katie, these are the kids who moved into Mrs. Templeton's house, Nicki and Shirley. And what's your friend's name?"

"Lisa."

"Yes, Lisa. Well, this is my girl, Katie. She's eight, too."

They looked at each other without comment. Lester sighed.

"Do you go to Watson School?" Katie asked.

"I don't know yet." Nicki knelt by her sister and joined in rubbing Lester's soft belly.

"You probably will. That's where I go. Are you going into third grade?"

"Yes."

"Then you'll be with me. We're going to have Mrs. Willowby for a teacher." She sat on the cement and scratched under the dog's chin.

"Are you in school yet?" Katie asked Shirley.

"Kindergarten," she answered.

"Mrs. Paulson. She's real nice. I had her. She has a cat in her class."

Lester's leg began to twitch in ecstasy, and they all laughed.

"Can Lester be my friend?" Shirley looked at Katie.

She shrugged. "I guess so. Why not?"

"Can Lester visit me?"

49

Mr. Leighton chuckled. "Like it or not, Lester probably *will* visit you. And Mrs. Templeton did *not* like it."

"You mean he used to visit Mrs. Templeton?"

"Something like that. Usually, he'd be chasing a cat or exploring. Our backyards meet at the corners, and there's a path that leads right to your back fence."

"There is?" Nicki's face lit up.

"Want me to show you?" Katie asked.

"Okay."

Katie turned and ran up her driveway, and Lester and the girls followed. They cut through the backyard and around the garage. And there, over an old split-log fence, was the gazebo. And there, sitting on the step of the gazebo and chewing honeysuckle, was Jeffrey.

He turned and stared at them. "Where have you been, Webber? I was worried that you left without letting me,—"

"Hi, Jeffrey." She cut him off and looked nervously at the others. They followed her over the fence, and she held her finger to her lips in a silent *shhhh* to Jeffrey.

Katie stayed at the fence with her hands on her hips. "Jeffrey Reynolds," she said, "I don't trust you. Have you still got those slugs?"

He stood up and grinned. "Swear I don't, Katie."

He shook his pockets and waved his fingers in the air. "Swear. No slugs."

Katie climbed hesitantly over the fence and walked to the gazebo.

Nicki stared at Jeffrey. "Slugs?" she asked.

"Mmmmm," he answered innocently. "Sometimes you can find them in compost heaps—when it starts to get dark. I can show you tonight, if you want, if you're still here."

"Where are you *going,* Nicki?" Shirley asked again. Shirley wasn't stupid. She knew something was going on.

"Nowhere, Shirley. I *told* you. Let's-play-hide-and-seek-Not-It!" she shouted in one breath.

"Not It!" yelled Jeffrey.

"Not It!"

"Not It!"

Shirley was It, and they scattered around the yard in all directions before she could even say one word.

Katie ran in the direction of her garage, Lisa ran towards the house, and when Jeffrey ran off in the direction of his raspberry shoots, Nicki dove in after him.

"Jeffrey. Jeffrey," she said in a low whisper. "I gotta talk to you."

He turned and unhooked his shirt from the thorns. "What's up? Problem with the plan?"

"Yeah. I don't think it's going to work. I don't want to go with Lisa."

"Won't she do it?"

"I didn't even ask her. I don't know. I just don't think I want to do it today."

He grinned. "Well, maybe we can work out a different plan. Something for later on."

"Yeah," she said, smiling. "Some other time. And tonight? Tonight do you think you could show me those slugs?"

"Sure." He was still smiling, and his teeth were just a little bit crooked, like new teeth. He had a good smile.

"You don't eat slugs, do you?" she asked.

"What are you, crazy?"

"Here I come, ready or not!" yelled Shirley.

8

Gazebo Races

When Lisa's mother came for her, Nicki stood at the curb and waved good-bye. Having Lisa visit her just wasn't the same as living at the old house, and she wasn't sure why. She only knew that she didn't like to hear about Lisa being in her old room, and it was strange to have Lisa playing along with her new friends here in her new neighborhood. It wasn't the same.

Nicki sat alone then on the step of the gazebo,

thinking. It was very quiet, almost dinnertime, but it was still a hot summer day, with locusts buzzing in the trees and the sun still shining.

She watched her father come out the back door. She sat very still and didn't let him know she was there. He walked from the house, then turned, and looked back at it. His back looked strong and straight. She could tell he really liked this house, and she looked at it with him. It wasn't so bad. Maybe she would grow to like it.

Her father walked slowly towards her, humming to himself. He stopped when he saw her.

"There you are, Nicki. Mom's looking for you, you know. It's almost time for dinner."

"Mmmmmm." She didn't move, and he sat down next to her, cupping his big hand over her small knee.

"How was your day with Lisa?"

"I don't know, Dad. I'm not sure we're best friends anymore. I met a new friend today, too, and I like her, and she's going to be in my class. And you know, I almost wanted Lisa to go home. And now Jeffrey is really my best friend, like Lisa used to be, but I don't think I can have two best friends, especially when one of them lives so far away." She sighed. "I get all mixed up."

Her father patted her knee. He understood. "So you came out here to sort it all out, huh?"

"Yeah."

"Reminds me of a poem I read once."

She waited.

" 'I am safe here,' " he said, " 'Not a friend in sight.' "

She laughed and felt very grown-up to understand a poem so completely.

"Well, kiddo, let's eat. Come on." He held out his hand to her, and they walked back to the house.

"Dad?"

"Yes?" He looked down at her.

"I was going to run away today. Go back to Lisa's and live in the old neighborhood."

"And?"

"I changed my mind for now."

He put his arm around her shoulder and patted her. "Good," he said. "I'm glad."

The table in the porch was set for dinner, and her mother was just carrying in a large bowl full of corn on the cob.

"There you are, Nicki. I was wondering where you'd gone. I thought maybe you and Jeffrey were off somewhere."

When her mother set the bowl on the table, Shirley stood on her chair and began lifting the ears of corn, one at a time with the tongs.

Suddenly Nicki noticed a quiet sound, like a crinkling noise that grew to a loud tapping. The porch roof began pounding with the sound of a summer shower. Her father sighed with pleasure and stood looking out into the yard. "Beautiful," he said. And then, all of a sudden, he looked back at them. His eyes grew wide, like Jeffrey's did sometimes.

"Gazebo races!" he shouted, and began tearing off his sneakers and socks.

"What?" Mrs. Bennet asked.

"Gazebo races!" he said again. "Come on. First one to the gazebo and back wins."

"John, don't be ridiculous. I'm just putting dinner on the table."

"Come on. Don't be left out. Gazebo races!" he yelled again.

Shirley giggled and ran to his side. He opened the porch door and propped it back. "Come on, Julie, Nicki. Don't be left out. Come on."

Nicki approached her father slowly. Her mother hesitated. "John, we'll get drenched."

"I know. That's the fun. Come on." He slipped her glasses off her nose and placed them on the porch ledge. Slowly, reluctantly, she began to slip her shoes off.

"John, this is ridiculous."

Nicki smiled at her father and slipped out of her sandals. "Ready?" she asked.

"On your mark!" he answered.

"Go!" Shirley cried, and the whole Bennet family tumbled off their back porch and tore across the lawn

in the pouring summer rain. They ran down the steps, over the slate walk, past the birdbath and the violets, around the yucca plant and into the gazebo, back out again, past the yucca, the violets, the birdbath, over the slate walk, and up the steps and in the back door.

Mr. Bennet won, and next came Nicki, and then Shirley. They stood dripping wet on the porch, laughing, and shaking themselves like wet dogs.

"Where's Mommy?" Shirley asked.

"I don't know." Mr. Bennet squinted out into the backyard. "Julie?" he called.

Over the pounding rain on the roof and the light rumble of thunder, they could hear their mother call.

"You didn't say to the gazebo and *back.*"

"Yes, I did."

"He did! He did!" the girls shouted.

"Mommy's stuck in the gazebo, gang. Let's go get her."

They tumbled out into the rain once again and met Mrs. Bennet halfway across the lawn. "All right. All right," she said. And they ran together back to the house.

"John, that was ridiculous. Dinner is on the table."

But she wasn't really angry. She was laughing.

Nicki looked at her family. They were funny, so wet and drippy. She stood looking at them, thinking about them, and it was at that very instant that Nicki knew that she was really home.

Tonight she and Jeffrey would find some slugs out

by the compost heap, and maybe Lester would come by, and they could all call for Katie and catch lightning bugs and put them in jars.

And maybe tomorrow she would unpack those boxes and fill up all the shelves and drawers in that dumb room of hers.

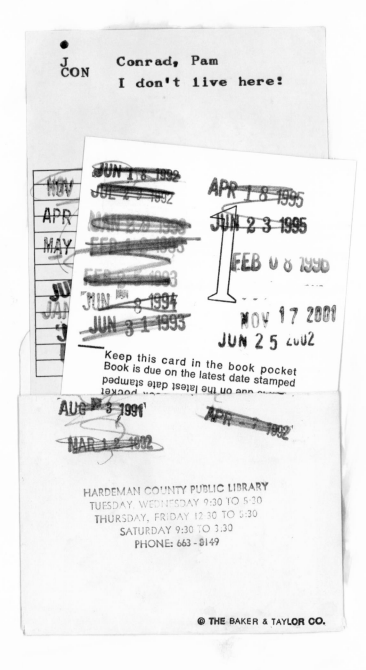

J
CON   Conrad, Pam
      I don't live here!

JUN 1 8 1992
JUL 2 3 1992   APR 1 8 1995
                     JUN 2 3 1995
                     FEB 0 8 1996

JUN   8 1994
JUN 3 1 1993   NOV 17 2001
                     JUN 25 2002

Keep this card in the book pocket
Book is due on the latest date stamped

AUG   3 1991   APR   1992
MAR 1 2 1992

HARDEMAN COUNTY PUBLIC LIBRARY
TUESDAY, WEDNESDAY 9:30 TO 5:30
THURSDAY, FRIDAY 12:30 TO 5:30
SATURDAY 9:30 TO 3:30
PHONE: 663 - 8149

© THE BAKER & TAYLOR CO.